The Story Machine
Tom McLaughlin

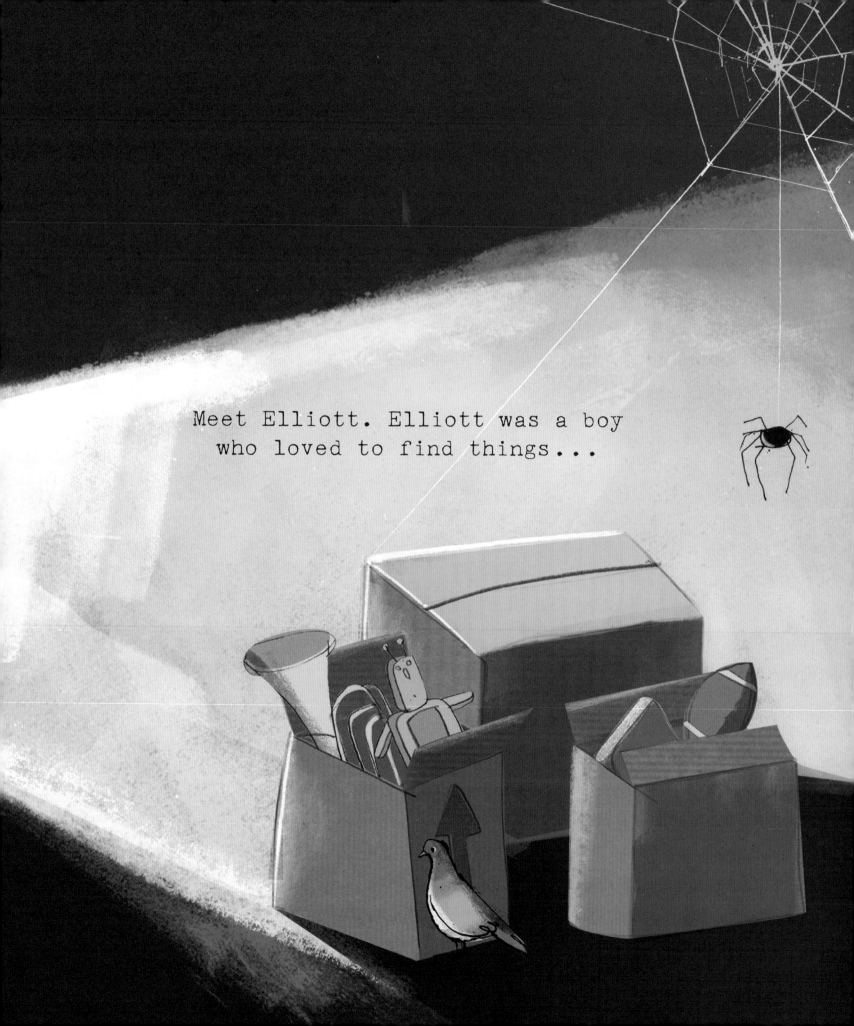

Meet Elliott. Elliott was a boy
who loved to find things...

And, one day, he found a machine.

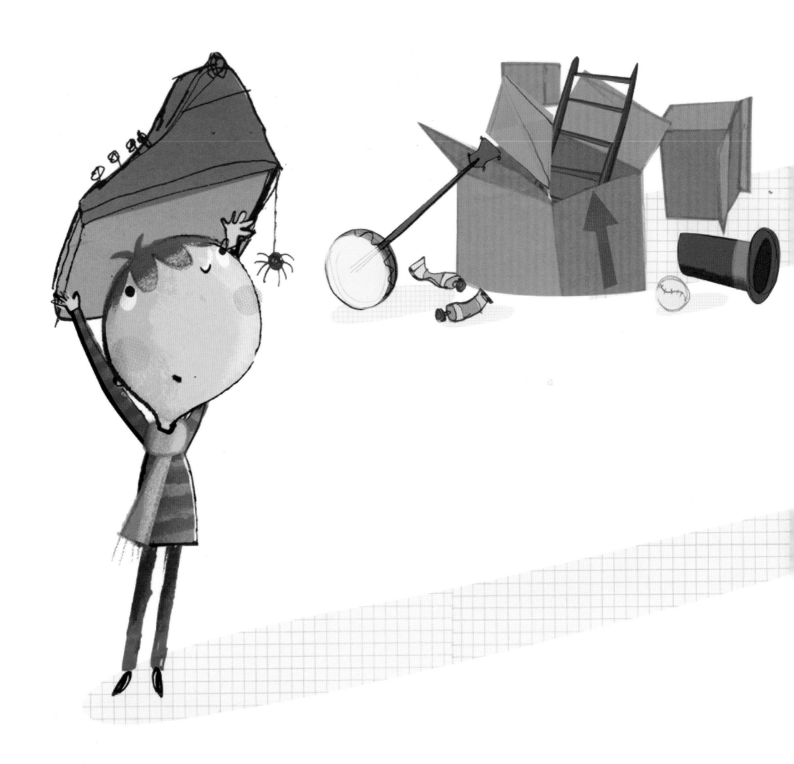

It didn't have an ON/OFF button
and it didn't even **bleep** or **buzz!**

Then, quite by accident, he made it work.

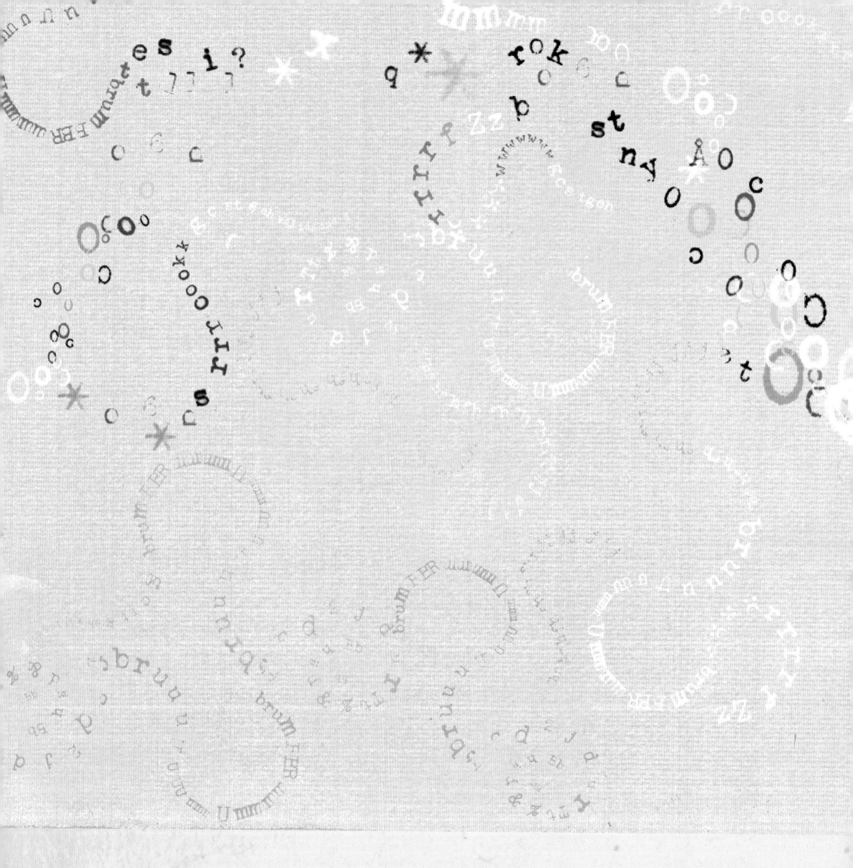

The machine made letters. And the letters made words. Perhaps it was a **story machine!**

Elliott, however, wasn't very good at letters.

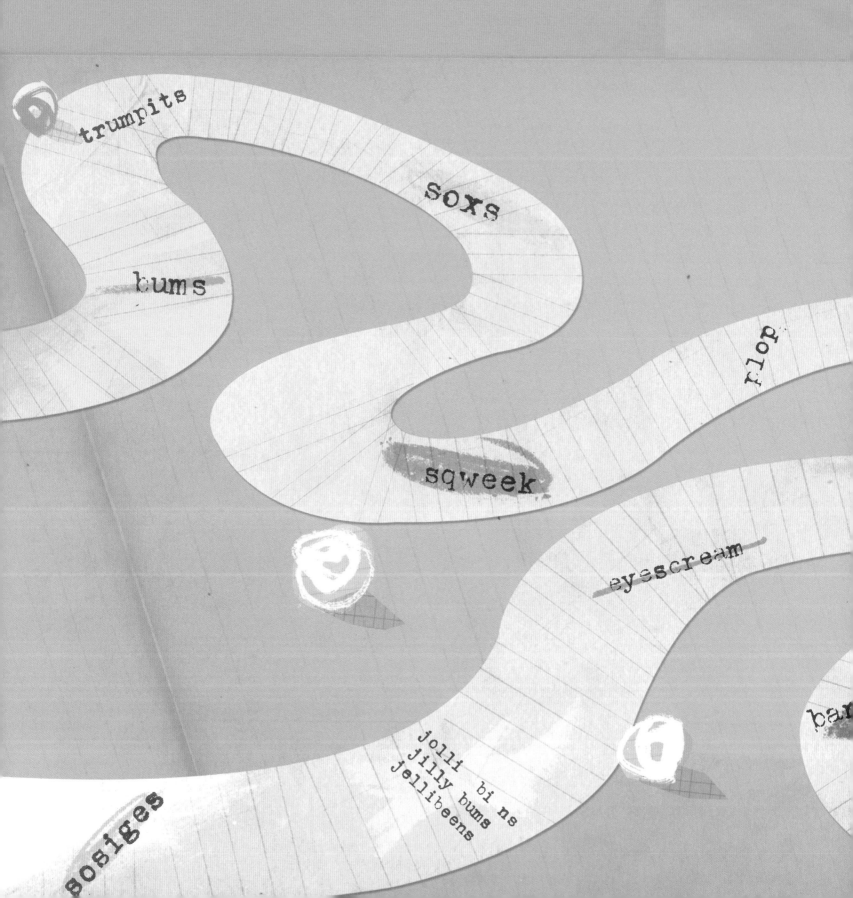

trumpits

soxs

bums

flop

sqweek

eyescream

bar

jolli bi ns
jilly bums
jellibeens

sosiges

He did his best, but he kept getting them all jumbled up.

wonce
up
onn a
tyme

sqweek

plop

zzz

Then Elliott noticed something
amongst the letters - a picture!

So Elliott began to make pictures...

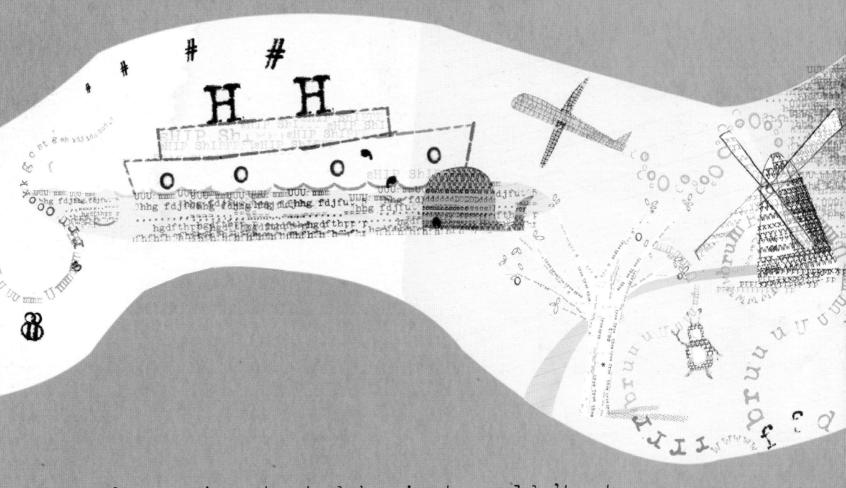

and once he started he just couldn't stop.

He made big pictures, small
pictures, busy pictures
and quiet pictures.

But the best thing about
all his pictures was that
they told a story.

Maybe it WAS a story
machine after all!

But it didn't take long for things to go wrong.

Elliott had used the story machine
so much it had begun to malfunction.

No more machine!

That meant no more pictures and no more stories.

Elliott was blue.

Until he found something else —
and that was when he realised
something very important...

It **wasn't** the machine that was making the stories...

My stories

Elliott

...it was him and he was
really rather good at it!

For Mum x
~ TM
With many thanks to Catherine Cartwright

Bloomsbury Publishing, London, New Delhi, New York and Sydney

First published in Great Britain in 2014 by Bloomsbury Publishing Plc
50 Bedford Square, London, WC1B 3DP

A CIP catalogue record for this book is available from the British Library

ISBN 978 1 4088 3933 1 (HB)
ISBN 978 1 4088 3934 8 (PB)
ISBN 978 1 4088 3932 4 (eBook)

Printed in China by C & C Offset Printing Co Ltd, Shenzhen, Guangdong

1 3 5 7 9 10 8 6 4 2

www.bloomsbury.com

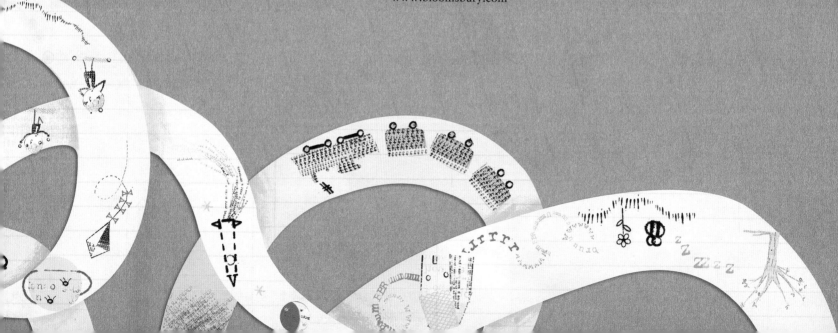